No Messin' with My Lesson

For my parents, Gladys and Steve—N.K.

For Julia Andrews—J&W

Text copyright © 2004 by Nancy Krulik. Illustrations copyright © 2004 by John and Wendy. All rights reserved. Published by Grosset & Dunlap, a division of Penguin Young Readers Group, 345 Hudson Street, New York, New York, 10014. GROSSET & DUNLAP is a trademark of Penguin Random House LLC. Manufactured in China

Library of Congress Cataloging-in-Publication Data

Krulik, Nancy E.
No messin' with my lesson / by Nancy Krulik ; illustrated by John & Wendy.
     p. cm. — (Katie Kazoo, switcheroo ; 11)
Summary: Katie's teacher, Mrs. Derkman, hopes to win the Teacher of the Year contest, but her chances do not look good when Katie turns into her teacher and cannot keep a class full of out-of-control third-graders in line.
     ISBN 0-448-43357-5 (pbk.)
[1. School—Fiction. 2. Teachers—Fiction. 3. Contests—Fiction. 4. Magic—Fiction.]   I. Title: No messin' with my lesson. II. John & Wendy. III. Title.
     PZ7.K9445No 2004
[Fic]—dc22

                                          2003016470

                          10 9 8 7 6 5 4 3 2 1

Proprietary ISBN 978-1-101-95134-7
Part of Boxed Set, ISBN 978-1-101-95128-6

No Messin' with My Lesson

by Nancy Krulik • illustrated by John & Wendy

Grosset & Dunlap

Chapter 1

"Cinderella, dressed in yellow. Went upstairs to kiss a fella. Made a mistake, and kissed a snake. How many doctors did it take? One, two, three . . ."

Katie Carew began to count as she turned her end of the double Dutch jump ropes. Her best friend, Suzanne Lock, was jumping between the ropes. Becky Stern was turning the other end.

Katie's other best friend, Jeremy Fox, was on the soccer field. He was kicking a ball around with Kevin Camilleri and Mandy Banks. George Brennan and Manny Gonzalez were on the swings, laughing at something.

Probably at one of George's jokes.

Everyone was having a great time.

The strange thing was, the only kids on the playground were the kids in class 3A. Everyone else had already gone in to start the school day. But no one had told the kids in Katie's class to stop playing and come inside.

"I wonder where Mrs. Derkman is?" Becky asked.

Usually, their teacher was on the playground before school began. When it was time for classes to start, she would blow her whistle, and the kids would line up to go into the building. But, this morning, Mrs. Derkman was nowhere to be found.

"Do you think we should go inside on our own?" Katie wondered. "School started five minutes ago."

"No way," Suzanne said between jumps. "I'm not going in there until someone tells me I have to."

Just then, Mr. Kane, the school principal, strolled onto the playground. "Class 3A," he called out. "You need to be in school now. Line up."

Katie immediately dropped her end of the double-Dutch ropes, and ran for the door. Suzanne tripped over the fallen ropes. *Plop*. She landed right on her rear end.

"Nice one, Suzanne," George Brennan teased. "How about giving us an instant replay?" He raced past her.

Suzanne glared at George.

As the kids lined up, Jeremy turned to Katie. "Do you think Mrs. Derkman is absent today?" he asked her.

Katie shook her head. "No way. Mrs. Derkman is *never* absent."

"I know," George agreed. "She's *always* at school. She's here when we get here in the morning, and she's here when we leave in the afternoon. I'd swear she lived in the school—if I didn't know she'd moved in next door to you, Katie Kazoo."

The other kids all looked sympathetically at Katie. Imagine having your teacher live right next door. Especially a strict teacher like Mrs. Derkman. Talk about bad luck!

"Maybe she's preparing a surprise for us in the classroom," Miriam Chan suggested.

"Oh, that would be awful," George moaned.

"How do you know?" Miriam asked him. "It could be something great."

"Any surprise Mrs. *Jerk*man could dream up would have to be bad," George told her. George did not like Mrs. Derkman very much.

"You children keep quiet as you walk down the hall," Mr. Kane warned as he led them inside. "The other classes are already busy learning."

×   ×   ×

Sure enough, Mrs. Derkman was there when the kids walked into the room. She was standing in the back of the room, looking through the lens of a video camera. The camera was planted firmly on top of a stand.

"What's that for?" Manny asked Mrs. Derkman.

"I'm going to tape our day," Mrs. Derkman explained.

"Why?" Manny asked.

Mrs. Derkman checked the lens one more time, and then walked to the front of the

room. "After school, I'm going to watch the tapes to see how I teach. That way, I can study what I'm doing right, and what I'm doing wrong. I can come up with ways to be a better teacher."

Katie looked at George. She could tell by the expression on his face that he was practically bursting with ideas for how Mrs. Derkman could be a better teacher. He opened his mouth to say something, but Mrs. Derkman shot him a look. George kept quiet.

"So you're going to watch the tapes the way a coach does after a football game, to see where the team went wrong," Jeremy said.

"Exactly," Mrs. Derkman told him. "You see, I've been entered in the Cherrydale Teacher of the Year Contest. One of the judges is going to come here and watch me teach. I want to make sure that I do my best."

"When is the judge coming?" Kevin asked.

Mrs. Derkman shrugged. "It's a surprise. I don't know when he will come or what he will grade me on."

The kids all stared at their teacher with amazement. Someone was going to give Mrs. Derkman a grade? Now that was a switch!

Mrs. Derkman walked over to the board and picked up a piece of chalk. "Now, just forget about the camera. Pretend it's not there. We have work to do."

Chapter 2

Mrs. Derkman may not have wanted anyone to think about the camera, but the kids couldn't help it. In fact, it was *all* they could think about.

"Who can tell me one problem the pioneers faced on their trip out west?" Mrs. Derkman asked the class during social studies. Many hands shot up. "Suzanne?" Mrs. Derkman said.

Usually, Suzanne would just give her answer from her seat. But not today. Suzanne stood up. She turned her face to the video camera, reached up, and wiped her forehead. Then she clutched her throat like she was in pain.

"During the summer months, the sun was strong, and sometimes the settlers didn't have enough water to drink," she moaned in a pained voice. "People actually died of thirst." She collapsed on her chair and threw her head back, pretending to faint.

The class began to laugh. A few kids actually applauded. Suzanne stood up and bowed.

"Watch out, Suzanne Superstar is ready for her close-up," Kevin teased.

"Suzanne, sit down," Mrs. Derkman said with a sigh. She looked at the class. "That's true. Both food and water were hard to come by. Now, does anyone else have a thought?"

Katie had some ideas about what problems the pioneers might have had. But she didn't raise her hand. She didn't want to risk giving a wrong answer. If she did, it would be on film forever!

But George wasn't afraid to be on camera. He raised his hand high.

Mrs. Derkman looked around the room to

see if anyone else had a hand up. But George was the only one. "George," Mrs. Derkman said finally.

Like Suzanne, George stood up and turned toward the camera. He held his pencil in his hand, and pretended it was a microphone. "Speaking of westward travel," he said. "Do you know why a drama teacher is like the pony express? Because he's a stage coach!"

A few kids laughed.

"Does anyone know who settled in the west before anyone else?" George continued.

"Who?" Manny asked.

"The sun!" George exclaimed.

The kids all laughed. "Tell another one, George," Kevin shouted.

George grinned. "Why did the criminal carry glue with him when he traveled out west?"

"Why?" Kevin shouted out.

"He wanted to stick up the passengers!"

Everyone laughed . . . everyone but Mrs.

Derkman, that is. "George, this is a classroom, not a comedy club," she scolded.

Mrs. Derkman did not look happy. Her face was all scrunched up, her glasses were halfway down her nose, and she'd squeezed her fist so tight that she'd snapped the chalk in half.

Katie glanced at the video camera in the back of the room. *I wonder how Mrs. Derkman will feel when she sees herself looking like that,* she thought to herself.

Mrs. Derkman didn't turn off her video camera at all during the day. And the more the camera recorded her, the stricter she got. During math time, the kids were all answering multiplication problems in their notebooks. Mrs. Derkman walked around the room, checking their work.

"Mandy, you know that by third grade all of your work has to be written in cursive," Mrs. Derkman scolded her.

Mandy seemed confused. "But this is math," she told her teacher. "There's no such thing as a cursive 7."

Mrs. Derkman continued walking around the room. She stopped in front of the third row. "Class, what is the rule about eating in this room?"

Katie looked around. She didn't see anyone eating anything.

"There is *no* eating in this classroom," Mrs. Derkman said, answering her own question. She strutted over to the window, and stared at

Speedy. "You've been here long enough to know that," she scolded the hamster.

Speedy took one look at Mrs. Derkman's angry face, and leaped away from his food bowl. He ran to hide inside his plastic tube.

The kids stared at their teacher. Worrying about the contest had obviously made her nuts!

"Boy, Mrs. Derkman is in a really bad mood today," Katie whispered to Kevin and Suzanne.

"I'll say," Suzanne agreed. "I think it has to do with that video camera. Some people act strange when there's a camera around."

Katie looked at "Suzanne Superstar" and laughed. "Gee, you think so?"

Chapter 3

Mrs. Derkman finally turned off her camera just before the bell rang. She relaxed right away. So did the kids. "Okay, children," the teacher said, a slight smile returning to her face. "Jeremy is now going to pass out this week's edition of the *Class 3A Times*."

Jeremy stood and proudly began to hand out the newspapers. He really loved being the editor of the class newspaper. "There are lots of great articles this week," he told the other kids. "Like the one about . . ."

"*My* new column is in there," Suzanne interrupted him. "It's called 'Ask Suzanne.' I know everyone is going to love it."

"I can't think of anything I'd want to ask her," Kevin whispered to George.

"I can," George answered. "I want to ask her to go away." Kevin and George laughed.

Suzanne scowled at them. "Shows what you know. I'm going to answer very important questions in my column. This week, I wrote about friendship."

Katie watched as Suzanne argued with

George and Kevin. "Are you sure giving Suzanne her own column was a good idea?" she whispered to Jeremy.

"I needed another article to fill the page," Jeremy admitted.

"But you know Suzanne. This could be trouble," Katie told him.

"It'll be okay," Jeremy answered. "Actually, her advice was pretty good. Read it."

Katie opened the newspaper to page three. Suzanne's column was at the top of the page. The question was:

Dear Suzanne,

My friend has a pair of pants that she loves to wear. But they are too tight and short on her, and I'm afraid they will split open! I want to tell her, but I don't want her to get mad at me.

Signed,
What Do I Do?

Suzanne had answered:

Dear What Do I Do?:
You should definitely tell your friend that her pants are too small. What if they split in the middle of recess? You will save her from embarrassment. Friends should always be honest with each other. When it comes to friendship, honesty is always the best policy.

"You see," Jeremy said after Katie had read the column. "Suzanne said people should be honest. What trouble could that cause?"

Katie shrugged. "I guess you're right," she agreed.

✕　✕　✕

That afternoon, Katie went home and did her homework. Then she went out into her yard to look for her cocker spaniel, Pepper. She found him next door, playing with Mrs. Derkman's dog, Snowball. They were both sniffing around the tomatoes and cucumbers in Mrs. Derkman's yard.

Katie figured Mrs. Derkman must not be in the yard. Otherwise, she would have shooed the dogs away from her vegetables. Mrs. Derkman loved her garden. She treated her plants like babies. She even sang to them!

Katie was right, Mrs. Derkman wasn't in the garden. But *Mr.* Derkman was. Katie was very surprised. She'd never seen her teacher's husband working in the garden before. He liked to lie in a big hammock under the tree while his wife dug up weeds and planted flowers. But, today, he was the one out there picking fresh cucumbers from the vine.

"Hi, Katie," Mr. Derkman greeted her.

"Hi," Katie replied. "I didn't know you liked to garden."

"I don't," Mr. Derkman admitted. "But my wife is so busy watching her videotapes that she doesn't have time to pick vegetables.

These cucumbers will rot on the vine if I don't bring them in."

"Mrs. Derkman sure is excited about the Teacher of the Year Contest," Katie said.

"I know," Mr. Derkman agreed. "I don't think I've ever seen her this way before. She says if she had only one wish, it would be to win Teacher of the Year."

Katie gulped slightly when Mr. Derkman said that. She knew a lot about wishes. Sometimes, when they came true, they caused a lot of trouble.

Katie learned all about wishes one evening after she'd had a really bad day. She'd lost the football game for her team, ruined her favorite pair of pants, and let out a big burp in front of the whole class. That night, Katie had wished she could be anyone but herself.

There must have been a shooting star overhead when she made that wish, because the very next day, the magic wind came and

20
X

turned Katie into Speedy the class hamster! All morning long, she gnawed on chew sticks and ran on a hamster wheel, until she finally turned back into herself!

The magic wind continued to come back again and again. It had already turned Katie into other kids, like Suzanne's baby sister Heather, and her friends Becky Stern and Jeremy Fox. Another time, it turned her into her dog Pepper—and she'd gotten into a huge argument with a particularly nasty squirrel. Once, the wind even turned her into Mr. Kane, the school principal. The whole school was almost destroyed that time!

Katie never knew when the magic wind would come back again. All she knew was that when it did, she was going to wind up getting into some sort of trouble—and so would the person or animal she turned into.

That was why Katie knew it was important to be careful what you wished for!

"Freddy Bear, you have a phone call," Mrs.

Derkman called suddenly from the front door.

Mr. Derkman looked up. "Coming, Snookums," he called back. He turned to Katie. "See you later, kiddo."

Katie sighed as Freddy Bear walked up to the house and went inside with his Snookums. She was *never* going to get used to having Mrs. Derkman as a next-door neighbor.

Chapter 4

"Are you sure it's safe to play in your yard today?" Suzanne asked Katie as they left school with Jeremy and George at the end of the next day. "I don't want to run into Mrs. Derkman."

"Mrs. Derkman's not going to be home yet," Katie assured Suzanne. "And when she does get home, she's not going to bother us. She'll be spending all her time inside watching her videotapes."

"I hope you're right," Jeremy said. "I don't like playing at your house very much now that Mrs. Derkman is your neighbor. I see enough of her at school."

Katie frowned. It made her feel bad that her best friend didn't want to play at her house.

"I was just being honest," Jeremy told her.

The kids began to walk in the direction of Katie's house. A minute later, Becky came up behind them.

Katie jumped. "Becky, you surprised me," Katie exclaimed.

"She didn't surprise *me*," Suzanne said. "She always shows up when Jeremy's around."

Jeremy and Becky both blushed. Then Jeremy looked angry.

"What?" Suzanne asked. "I was just being honest."

Jeremy scowled at Suzanne, but said nothing. What could he say? He was the editor of the class paper. It had been his idea to print Suzanne's advice column in the first place.

"Hi, kids," Mrs. Carew greeted them as they walked up the walkway to Katie's house.

"I hope you're hungry. I've got lots of choco-late chip cookies." She held out a large plate.

Becky grabbed a chocolate chip cookie and took a bite. "This is pretty good, Mrs. Carew," she said. "But my mom makes them much better. Hers are chewier, and they have a lot more chips."

Katie's mom didn't know what to say. The kids all stared at Becky with surprise.

Becky shrugged. "I was just being . . ."

"Honest," George, Jeremy, Suzanne, and Katie finished her sentence for her.

The other kids seemed to like the cookies a lot. They chowed down on them. When they were finished eating, Katie's mom took the empty plate into the house. "Don't stay out here too long," she warned Katie as she went inside. "You have to do your homework."

Katie nodded. "We don't have too much," she assured her mother.

"Does anyone else think Mrs. Derkman is acting especially weird lately?" Suzanne asked the others once Mrs. Carew was gone and they were alone.

"I'll say," Becky agreed. "Did you hear her yelling at Speedy yesterday?"

"Poor little hamster," Katie agreed.

George stood up. He wrinkled his brow and scrunched up his mouth. He pretended to look through a pair of glasses.

"Speedy, there will be no scratching in this classroom," he said, imitating Mrs. Derkman. "And there will be no running on the hamster wheel. There is no running in the classroom at all. Save that for the playground."

Katie giggled.

"No laughing, Katie," George said in a stern voice. "School is not supposed to be fun."

"It sure wasn't fun today," Jeremy said. "I was afraid to breathe."

"That's the new rule," George said. "From now on, students are only allowed to breathe during lunch."

The kids all laughed. George was imitating their teacher perfectly.

"That's pretty good, George," Jeremy giggled.

"Yeah, you sound just like Mrs. *Jerk*man," Suzanne agreed.

Suddenly, the kids heard footsteps on the sidewalk. They stopped laughing and turned around.

"Uh-oh," Becky murmured.

Mrs. Derkman was standing in her drive-way. She had just arrived home from school. Katie was sure her teacher had heard them talking about her.

"We're in trouble now," George whispered.

But Mrs. Derkman didn't say a word. She just turned, and sadly went into her house.

Chapter 5

When Katie arrived at school the next morning, everyone was upset. And not because of how strict Mrs. Derkman had become. The kids were fighting with one another—and it was all because of Suzanne's advice column.

"I don't know what your problem is," Katie heard Jeremy say to Manny. "All I said was that you don't run fast enough to be on our team in the relay race."

"That's really mean," Manny replied.

"I'm just being honest," Jeremy told him. "You're not a fast runner. As your friend, I owe it to you to tell you the truth."

Jeremy and Manny weren't the only ones having an argument. George and Kevin weren't getting along too well, either.

"Here's my new joke," George said. "What do you call a jogging almond?"

"What?" Kevin asked.

"A health nut!" George laughed, but Kevin didn't.

George looked at him strangely. "Don't you get it?"

Kevin nodded. "I get it. I just don't think it's funny."

George's eyes opened wide. "What do you mean it's not funny?" he demanded.

"Hey, don't get mad at me," Kevin insisted. "I'm just being honest."

George stormed away.

It wasn't only the boys who were having trouble with the truth. As she turned away from George, Katie spotted Zoe Canter sitting under a tree. She was crying. Katie walked over to see what was wrong.

"What's up, Zoe?" she asked.

"Miriam and Mandy just told me not to meet them at the mall on Saturday," Zoe told Katie between sobs.

"Why would they do that?"

Zoe shrugged. "They said they *honestly* wanted some time alone. Now *I* have nothing to do. I can't believe they're leaving me out like this."

Katie sighed. The kids were taking Suzanne's advice too seriously. Sometimes, the truth hurt. Katie decided to talk to Suzanne about it. Maybe her friend could write a new article for next week's paper— one that was about not hurting other people's feelings.

But, before Katie could speak to Suzanne, Mrs. Derkman blew her whistle three times. It was time to go inside.

The kids were still arguing as they walked into the classroom, put their homework in the bin, and hung up their jackets. As soon as everyone was in their seats, Mrs. Derkman called for quiet.

"You have to be especially well-behaved now," Mrs. Derkman reminded the class. "The judges for the Teacher of the Year Contest will be here any day now. It could be today, tomorrow, or the next day."

"You mean we have to be good for three whole days?" George asked. "I don't know if I can do that."

Mrs. Derkman didn't say anything. She didn't have to. The look on her face was enough to make George be quiet.

"She's in a bad mood again!" Suzanne mumbled under her breath.

Unfortunately, she wasn't so quiet that Mrs. Derkman couldn't hear her. The teacher's face got even more angry. She stared at the second row. "Did you say something . . . Katie?" she asked.

"No," Katie assured her honestly.

"Yes, you did," Mrs. Derkman said. "I heard you."

"It wasn't me," Katie insisted. "It was . . ." Katie stopped herself. She didn't want to squeal on Suzanne.

"There is no rudeness allowed in this class. Go down and sit in Mr. Kane's office," Mrs. Derkman told her. "You need to spend some time thinking about how your words affect others."

"But I . . ."

"No buts, Katie. I said go to Mr. Kane's office."

Katie could feel tears welling up in her eyes. She was being punished, and she hadn't done anything wrong. That was the worst feeling in the world.

The hallway was empty as Katie made her way toward the principal's office. Suddenly, she felt a cool, gentle breeze blowing on the back of her neck. She looked up to see if a window was open. But all the windows in the hallway were shut tight. So were the doors. The breeze wasn't coming from outside.

Oh, no! The magic wind was back!

Within seconds, the wind began to swirl around Katie like a wild tornado, blowing her hair all around her face. Katie shut her eyes tight. The wind grew stronger—so strong that Katie thought it would blow her away!

And then it stopped. Just like that. The magic wind was gone.

Which could only mean one thing. Katie had turned into someone else. The question was, who?

Chapter 6

"What page should we turn to, Mrs. Derkman?" Katie heard someone ask.

Slowly, she opened her eyes. She looked around. The room was very familiar. There was a hamster by the window, rows of desks, and a bulletin board that said "Math Rules!" on the back wall.

Katie knew this classroom very well. This was her classroom. Class 3A.

Okay, so now she knew where she was. But she didn't know *who* she was.

"Mrs. Derkman," Mandy said again. "You didn't tell us what page to turn to."

All eyes seemed to be on Katie. Katie looked down at the floor. There were sensible leather shoes on her feet. She was wearing a black skirt that just covered her knees, and a long-sleeved white blouse. Katie would never wear boring clothes like that.

But Mrs. Derkman would!

Oh, no! Katie had turned into her teacher!

Katie gulped. She didn't know anything about being a teacher. She didn't even know what book the kids had on their desks. She'd been in the hall when Mrs. Derkman had started the lesson.

But there was one person who knew how to be Mrs. Derkman. And he did it perfectly. Katie thought back to yesterday, when George had imitated Mrs. Derkman. She tried to do what he had done. She wrinkled her brow, and scrunched up her mouth. She looked down through Mrs. Derkman's half-glasses.

"Mrs. Derkman, do you have a toothache?" Miriam Chan asked her.

Katie sighed. Obviously, she didn't look as much like Mrs. Derkman as she'd thought. She was never going to be able to teach her friends anything.

But she had to do *something* with the class. Otherwise, they were sure to figure out that she wasn't really their teacher. Katie thought for a moment. Then she came up with a plan.

"Class, I've changed my mind," Katie said finally. "We're going to start the day with free reading. Everyone, take out your books."

The kids all looked at one another. They never started the day with free reading.

"What are you waiting for?" Katie scolded them, trying to sound like Mrs. Derkman. "Take out your books."

The kids did as they were told. As they began to read, Katie sat down at Mrs. Derkman's desk. The blue notebook Mrs. Derkman always carried was sitting right there. Maybe there was some clue in there about what Mrs. Derkman had wanted to teach today.

Katie opened the notebook. On the first page was a list of the kids in class 3A. Next to each of the names was a row of letters. She looked at the first one.

Kevin Camilleri: B, B+, A, C

Katie slammed the book shut. The blue book was Mrs. Derkman's grade book. Katie didn't want to look at her friends' test grades. Well, maybe she *wanted* to, but she knew she shouldn't. Grades were private.

Katie sat back in Mrs. Derkman's big, wooden chair and sighed. Her only hope was that the magic wind would blow again and turn her back into herself before she actually had to teach anything.

The trouble with that plan was that the magic wind only came when Katie was alone. Teachers were never alone in school. There were always kids around them. Teachers never even got to go to the bathroom. At least, Katie had never seen one get up to go.

As Katie thought about her big problem, she heard whispering. She looked out at her friends. Becky was whispering something to Jeremy.

"Becky!" Katie scolded her, trying to sound like their teacher. "We are reading now."

Becky looked back down at her book.

One minute later, Katie watched as a note flew across the room and landed on Zoe's desk. Katie knew that Mrs. Derkman would take the note and read it out loud. But Katie couldn't be that mean.

"Zoe, throw that in the garbage right now," she said instead.

Zoe stood up and did as she was told.

After that, everyone was quiet. At least for a few minutes. Then Kevin started drumming his fingers on his desk. *Tap tap tap. Tap tap tap.*

George began humming as he read. *Hmmm. Hmmm. Hmmm.*

The sound was driving Katie crazy. "Kevin! George!" she shouted, her voice suddenly sounding shrill and sharp. "This isn't music class. There's no singing or drumming here. You need to be quiet."

"Boy, Mrs. *Jerk*man is really mean today," Mandy whispered to Suzanne.

Katie frowned. She hadn't been trying to be mean. She'd just been trying to make sure everyone could read. Obviously, free reading time wasn't working. Katie was going to have to teach a lesson whether she liked it or not.

She wrote a division problem on the board.

$$3\overline{)15}$$

"Okay, class, put away your books," Katie said. "We're going to have a math lesson. Today, we will review division."

It was better to review something than to teach something new. After all, Katie didn't know anything new.

"Fifteen divided by three is five," Jeremy said.

"Very good," Katie agreed.

"That's not good," Suzanne interrupted.

"It's not?" Katie asked her.

"No. He called out. We're not allowed to call out," Suzanne explained.

Oops. Suzanne was right. Mrs. Derkman did not allow anyone to answer a question without raising his or her hand.

"So what?" Becky butted in. "He was right, wasn't he?"

"But he didn't follow the rules," Suzanne said.

"Well, neither did you," Jeremy told her. "You just called out, too."

Before Katie could say anything, Mr. Kane entered the room. He was followed by a stranger in a blue suit. The stranger was carrying a notebook. The two men walked quietly to the back of the room. Mr. Kane smiled and whispered something to the visitor.

Suddenly, Katie had a horrible thought. The stranger must be the judge for the Teacher of the Year Contest. He was going to judge Mrs. Derkman right now. And Mrs. Derkman wasn't even there!

This was *so* not good.

Chapter 7

There was nothing Katie could do but keep on teaching. Quickly, she scribbled another division problem on the board.

"Who can answer this question?" Katie asked the class. "What is twenty-seven divided by nine?" Lots of kids raised their hands. "Kevin?" Katie said.

"Four," Kevin said confidently.

Katie nodded and turned to the blackboard. She began to write another problem on the board.

But, before she could, Mandy raised her hand. "Mrs. Derkman?"

"Yes, Mandy?" Katie asked.

"Kevin's not right," Mandy told her. "Twenty-seven divided by nine equals three."

"It does not," Kevin argued.

"Sure it does," Mandy told him. "Because nine times three equals twenty-seven."

"Uh, very good, Mandy. I must have heard Kevin incorrectly," muttered Katie.

Mandy smiled at Katie. "I know all my times tables perfectly, Mrs. Derkman."

"You're stuck-up," Kevin said.

"That's not nice," Miriam chimed in.

"I'm just being honest, like Suzanne said we should be," Kevin told her.

"You're jealous because I'm better in math and sports than you are," Mandy told him.

"You're not so great, Mandy," Becky butted in. "You're not the best soccer player in the class. Jeremy is. And that's the honest truth!"

Katie knew she had to calm the kids down. But how? "You guys, come on," she said helplessly.

No one listened to her. Instead, the

arguing got worse. "Becky, you always say things like that," Suzanne said. "Everyone knows you have a big, fat crush on Jeremy."

Jeremy blushed. He turned to Suzanne. "Well, as long as we're being honest," he said, "you look like a banana in that yellow dress!"

Suzanne gulped. No one had ever said anything bad about her clothes before. "I do not!" she shouted. "This is a very cool outfit. Everybody thinks so."

"I don't," Becky said. "I think Jeremy is right. You *do* look like a banana."

"You don't know anything about style," Suzanne shouted back.

"You think you're the best at everything," Becky said to Suzanne.

"I do not!" Suzanne shouted back.

"I'm just telling the truth," Becky said. "But you're not the best. Can you do this?" Becky leaped out of her seat and did a back flip. She landed on the floor in a split.

Katie looked helplessly at the class. She

gulped. Mr. Kane was still standing there in the back of the room. But he didn't look happy anymore. His face was beet red, and his eyes were bulging. A vein was throbbing at the top of his bald head.

The principal couldn't take the arguing anymore. He took a step toward the front of the room and opened his mouth to speak.

But, before Mr. Kane could say a word, the judge tapped him on the shoulder. He whispered something in the principal's ear. Mr. Kane whispered something back. The judge shook his head.

Mr. Kane threw his hands up in the air. "This is a disaster!" he said. Then he stormed out of the room. The door slammed shut behind him.

The judge did not leave the room. He stayed to watch what would happen next. From the look on his face, Katie could tell he was very disappointed at the way things were going. So, Katie did a very un-Derkman thing.

She leaped up on a desk and whistled—loud.

The kids stopped talking and stared at their teacher. Mrs. Derkman had never done anything like that before.

"Okay, everyone sit down," Katie said. "This is not a nice way to act."

"But we're just being honest," Suzanne said. "Friends have to be honest with each other."

Katie nodded. "There's a difference between being honest, and being mean," she said. "I think maybe you were using Suzanne's advice column as an excuse to be mean. And that is totally not okay."

Totally not okay? The kids all stared at one another. Mrs. Derkman never spoke like that.

"I think it's okay to be honest if you're trying to help someone. But you should do that in private. And sometimes it's better to keep quiet than to say something that'll hurt your friend's feelings. You guys didn't care whose feelings you hurt."

The class stared at her. Mrs. Derkman never called her class *you guys*. She always called them children or students. Mrs. Derkman sure was acting strange.

But she was right. And the kids knew it.

At first, no one said anything. Then, Mandy turned to Kevin. "I guess it wasn't nice to say you weren't good in math or sports. You're really good at basketball."

Kevin nodded. "Thanks. And you're amazing in math. I guess I was just mad that I got the problem wrong."

Katie smiled at the class. "I think we should put our math books away. I have a better lesson." She began to hand out pieces of paper. "I want each of you to make a list of everyone in this class. Then I want you to write one nice thing about each of your class-mates."

"I'll start with George. He's really funny," Jeremy said as he began his list.

"Suzanne has great style," Becky said, writing on her paper. "And Jeremy is an awesome soccer player."

"Zoe is a terrific artist," Miriam added as she wrote.

"Manny has good handwriting," Suzanne murmured as she began to make up her list.

Before long, the kids were all busy writing. Katie looked back at the contest judge. He seemed really happy to see the students interested in their work!

But would that be enough for Mrs. Derkman to win the contest?

Chapter 8

Somehow, Katie managed to get through the rest of the day as Mrs. Derkman. When school ended, she was really tired. Keeping a whole class of third-graders busy and out of trouble wasn't easy. Katie just wanted to go home and relax.

But which home should she go to? She couldn't go to her house. Not as long as she looked like Mrs. Derkman. As she walked home, Katie began to worry. This was the longest she'd ever spent as someone else.

Katie hoped the magic wind would come back soon. If it didn't, Katie might wind up eating dinner with Freddy Bear Derkman!

Just then, the door to Mrs. Derkman's house swung open. But it wasn't the magic wind that did it. It was Mr. Derkman.

"Surprise, Snookums," he called out as he walked toward Katie. "I got out of work early."

"Oh, hello, Mr. Derk . . ." Katie began. "I mean, Freddy Bear."

Mr. Derkman reached out his arms. "How about a kissy-poo, Snookums?" he asked. He puckered up his lips for a big smooch.

Yuck! Katie certainly didn't want to give Freddy Bear a kissy-poo! But how could she avoid it?

"Ruff! Ruff!" Just then, Pepper came running over to Katie. He rubbed his back up against her knees and barked happily. Katie bent down and scratched him gratefully behind the ears.

Pepper licked Katie on the nose. He knew she wasn't *really* Mrs. Derkman. Pepper would know his Katie anywhere.

But Snowball didn't know who Katie was. She ran up and sniffed at Katie. Then she looked up, confused. This person looked like her human mommy, she smelled like her human mommy, but somehow Snowball knew that she wasn't Mrs. Derkman. Snowball began to bark wildly.

"I guess she's hungry," Mr. Derkman said. "I'll take her inside and give her some food."

As Mr. Derkman went back into the house, Katie breathed a sigh of relief. Thank goodness for dogs. But Katie knew she couldn't avoid kissing Mr. Derkman forever—at least not as long as she was *Mrs.* Derkman.

Just then, Katie felt a cool breeze blowing on the back of her neck. Katie looked up at the trees. The leaves were still. She looked down at the grass. Not a blade was moving.

The magic wind was back.

Within seconds, the wind was swirling around her like a giant tornado. Katie felt like she could be blown away at any minute. Quickly, she grabbed onto a tree and shut her eyes, tight.

And then it stopped. Just like that.

Slowly, Katie opened her eyes. She looked down at her feet. The sensible leather shoes were gone, and there were platform sneakers in their place. Instead of a skirt, Katie was wearing jeans, with laces down the sides. She put her hands to her face. She wasn't wearing glasses anymore.

Just then, Katie's mother came outside.

"There you are, Katie," her mother said. "How was school?"

Katie smiled brightly. She was back! "School was okay," she said.

"Anything exciting happen?"

Katie knew she couldn't tell her mother what had happened today. Her mother wouldn't believe her. Katie wouldn't have believed it either, if it hadn't happened to her.

"Nah," Katie said finally. "It was just a regular day."

Chapter 9

Most of the kids in class 3A were already on the playground by the time Katie arrived at school the next day. But they weren't playing or running around. They were busy watching as Mr. Kane spoke to Mrs. Derkman. The principal did not look happy.

"Your class was out of control yesterday," he told Mrs. Derkman.

"I know," Mrs. Derkman admitted sadly. "I'm not sure how that happened."

"What do you mean?" Mr. Kane asked.

"Well, I mean, I know what happened. But it's almost like that wasn't me up there in the front of the room." Mrs. Derkman sounded very confused.

"It certainly looked like you," Mr. Kane told her.

"It was me," Mrs. Derkman said. "I mean, at least I think it was. But I didn't feel like me. Oh, I don't know what to think."

Mr. Kane shook his head. "Well, it doesn't matter now. It doesn't seem as though you'll be winning the Teacher of the Year Award this time around."

Mrs. Derkman looked like she was about to cry.

✕ ✕ ✕

"Boy, Mrs. Jerkman looks unhappy. Mr. Kane must be really mad at her," George told the other kids.

"That's not nice, George," Katie said.

"What?" George asked her.

"Calling her Mrs. Jerkman," Katie told him.

"We always call her that," Kevin said.

"It's still not nice."

The other kids stared at Katie. *Was she*

really standing up for their teacher?

"Mrs. Derkman isn't nice to us, either," Suzanne reminded Katie. "She's very strict. And she gets mad a lot."

"That's because we're not always very good in class," Katie reminded her. "We pass notes and whisper."

"Yeah, well, Mrs. Derkman writes notes, too," George argued. "She sent one to my mother last week. And it wasn't a nice note, either!"

Katie rolled her eyes. "What about yesterday?" she asked the kids. "Everybody was yelling at each other during math. The judge from that contest saw the whole fight."

"How do you know what happened?" George asked Katie. "You were in Mr. Kane's office all day."

Of course, Katie *had* been in the classroom. But she couldn't tell the other kids that. So, instead, she said, "I heard about it. It sounds like everyone was mad at each other."

"But we made up," Mandy told Katie. "And we wrote nice things about each other. The judge from the contest saw us doing that, too."

"Yeah, he seemed happy about that," Miriam added. "He was really smiling when he left."

Katie shrugged. "But he wasn't happy enough to make Mrs. Derkman the Teacher of the Year. She really wanted that award. We blew it for her."

"She blew it for herself," George said. "She jumped up on a desk and whistled. If I did that, she'd send me to the principal's office."

"Yeah," Kevin agreed.

Katie gulped. George was right. Maybe if she hadn't jumped up on that desk, Mrs. Derkman would have had a chance. Now Katie felt worse than ever. "Mrs. Derkman deserves that award. She works really hard. Her feet hurt at the end of the day," Katie insisted.

Jeremy looked at her strangely. "How do you know?" he asked.

"I . . . er . . . well, she stands up at the board so much, I just figure they would hurt," Katie said quickly. "Besides, Mrs. Derkman might not be the nicest teacher in the school, but we learn a lot with her. We're the only class who studied geography this year. And we're the only ones who got to do research projects on things that interested us."

The kids couldn't argue with that. They *had* learned a lot in third grade. For a minute, everyone was quiet.

"We should make it up to her," Mandy said finally.

"I'm going to try to be extra good today," Miriam vowed.

"Me, too," Zoe agreed.

"I guess I will, too," Kevin said. He turned to Suzanne. "That means you can't ask me to pass any notes to Katie."

"I won't," Suzanne agreed. "I'm not going to write any notes today."

It sounded like everyone was going to try to make Mrs. Derkman happy today. Everyone except George, that is. He hadn't said anything about being good in class. All the kids turned to look at him.

"Why are you all staring at me?" George asked.

"Because we want you to be nice to Mrs. Derkman today," said Miriam.

"Yeah," agreed Zoe.

"That means no jokes, George," Kevin said, laughing.

"Oh, boy," replied George.

"George, please be nice to Mrs. Derkman today," Katie pleaded.

George sighed. "Do I have to?"

"Come on, George," Kevin said. "If I have to be good, so do you. Besides, it will really freak her out if *you're* good."

George smiled brightly. He liked that idea.

"Okay," he agreed. "But just for today."

Katie looked at her friends and grinned. Mrs. Derkman wasn't going to get a big trophy. But she was going to have an easy day teaching class 3A. Surely that would make her happy.

Chapter 10

The kids were all true to their word. No one spoke without raising their hand. No one passed any notes in class. No one chewed gum, or stared at the clock, or doodled in their notebook.

But Mrs. Derkman didn't seem to notice how well her students were behaving. She just frowned and sighed a lot.

At the end of the day, Mrs. Derkman told the kids to open their free reading books. Usually, Mrs. Derkman watched the kids as they read to make sure no one misbehaved. But today, Mrs. Derkman stared out the window. She didn't seem to notice the class at all.

Suddenly, there was a knock at the door. Mr. Kane walked into the classroom. He was carrying a gold trophy.

Mrs. Derkman turned and looked at him in confusion. "What is this for?" she asked. "I don't understand."

"This is for you," Mr. Kane said. "It's from the Cherrydale Teacher of the Year Award Committee."

"But you said I didn't win," Mrs. Derkman reminded him.

"You didn't win Teacher of the Year. That went to a teacher at the middle school."

"Then what is that trophy for?" Mrs. Derkman asked him.

"It's a special award," Mr. Kane said. "It's the first time they've ever given it."

"What's it for?" Katie asked excitedly, forgetting that she wasn't supposed to call out in class.

Mrs. Derkman must have forgotten that rule, too. She didn't yell at Katie. Instead she asked, "Yes, what is it for?"

Mr. Kane looked at the plaque on the base of the trophy. *"This award is presented to Mrs. Barbara Derkman for her creative lesson on consideration and caring for one another's feelings,"* he read.

Katie smiled. She *knew* the judge had liked that part of the class.

Mr. Kane gave Mrs. Derkman her trophy. "The contest judge called to tell me he liked the way you were able to get your students to apologize and see the good in one another," he said. Then he added, "Asking the students to write nice things about each of their classmates was a great idea."

"Oh," Mrs. Derkman said. "I guess you're talking about that pile of papers on my desk."

"You sound like you don't know where those papers came from," Mr. Kane laughed.

Mrs. Derkman didn't say anything. The truth was, she *wasn't* completely sure about anything that had happened yesterday.

"Anyway, he was really impressed with the way you were able to talk to your students on their own level. He said you almost sounded like a third-grader yourself."

Katie choked back a laugh. Mrs. Derkman had sounded like a third-grader yesterday because she *was* a third-grader. But, of course, Katie was the only one who knew that. And she wasn't going to tell anyone.

"I'm sure your class is very proud of you,"

Mr. Kane told Mrs. Derkman. He started to clap for her. The kids clapped, too.

"I'm proud of them," Mrs. Derkman told Mr. Kane. "I may not be the teacher of the year, but 3A is definitely Cherrydale's Class of the Year. To celebrate, I'm not giving any homework today. I want you all to go home and play!"

The class cheered even louder.

"Does this mean we can stop being good now?" George whispered to Katie as the class cheered for their teacher.

Before Katie could answer him, she felt a cool breeze on the back of her neck. *Oh, no! Was the magic wind back again? Was it going to change her into someone else right here in front of all her friends?* The magic wind had never come when other people were around before. But there was a first time for everything.

"Katie, you'd better close that window," Mrs. Derkman said. "That wind isn't good for

Speedy. He might catch a cold."

Katie breathed a sigh of relief. If Mrs. Derkman felt the breeze, then the magic wind hadn't come back. At least not right now. But it could come back anytime, and turn Katie into anyone.

She hurried to close the window. She never knew who the wind might turn her into next. It could turn her into Speedy again! And the last thing Katie would want to be turned into was a hamster with a cold.

For now, though, Katie was herself. And that made her very happy. After all, of all the people the magic wind had turned her into so far, Katie Carew was the one she liked best.

An Apple for the Teacher

This apple graham cracker snacker is a snack even Mrs. Derkman can't resist.

You will need:
2 red delicious apples
1 cup lemon juice
$^1/_2$ cup chunky peanut butter
2 tablespoons honey
$^1/_2$ tsp. cinnamon
6 whole graham crackers
A helpful adult

Here's what you do: Ask an adult to core the apples and cut each one in half. Then cut each half into three wedges (so you have 12 apple wedges). Dip the wedges in lemon juice to keep them from browning. Place the wedges in a single layer on a microwavable plate or baking dish. Cover the wedges loosely with waxed paper. Ask an adult to microwave the wedges on high for $3 \frac{1}{2}$–4 minutes (until apples are tender). Drain the apples on a paper towel.

In a small bowl, combine the peanut butter, honey, and cinnamon. Snap the graham crackers in half to make 12 squares. Spread a layer of the peanut butter mixture on each of the six graham cracker squares. Top each square with the remaining graham cracker squares to make sandwiches.

Makes six snacks.

No Bones About It

For Mandy and Ian,
great kids, no bones about it!—N.K.

To Ron and Kellie,
light box builders extraordinaire!—J&W

Text copyright © 2004 by Nancy Krulik. Illustrations copyright © 2004 by John and Wendy. All rights reserved. Published by Grosset & Dunlap, a division of Penguin Young Readers Group, 345 Hudson Street, New York, New York, 10014. GROSSET & DUNLAP is a trademark of Penguin Random House LLC.
Manufactured in China

Library of Congress Cataloging-in-Publication Data is available.

10 9 8 7 6 5 4 3 2 1

Proprietary ISBN 978-1-101-95134-7
Part of Boxed Set, ISBN 978-1-101-95128-6

No Bones About It

by Nancy Krulik • illustrated by John & Wendy

Grosset & Dunlap

Chapter 1

"Ouch!" Katie Carew shouted. She turned around and stared at Kevin Camilleri. "Stop kicking the seat!"

Kevin grinned at Katie. "I didn't do it. George did."

George Brennan was sitting next to Kevin on the school bus. The kids in class 3A were on their way to the Cherrydale Museum of Natural History for a field trip.

"It wasn't me," George assured Katie.

"It must have been a ghost," Kevin joked.

Katie sighed. "I don't care who it was. Just stop kicking."

As Katie turned back around in her seat,

one of her best friends, Suzanne Lock, let out a yelp.

"George, keep your disgusting hands off my ponytail!" she shouted. "It took me hours to get it right. You're going to ruin it."

"You mean you *meant* for it to look like that?" George asked.

Suzanne looked at Katie. "Boys!" she huffed. "They're all pains in the neck."

"Jeremy's not a pain," Katie pointed out.

Suzanne rolled her eyes. "He's *your* friend, Katie. Not mine."

It was true. Jeremy Fox was Katie's other best friend. But he and Suzanne did not get along at all.

Katie looked across the aisle. Jeremy was sitting next to Manny Gonzalez. They were making bunny ears over Becky Stern's head. Katie was glad Suzanne didn't see them. It would only prove her point.

"Hey, Jeremy! Manny! Watch this," George called out. He stuck his tongue out at a

car that was passing by.

"How about this?" Manny said. He squashed his nose and mouth up against the bus window.

"You guys better stop that," Katie warned them. "If Mrs. Derkman catches you, you'll be in big trouble!"

"She's all the way in the front of the bus," George said. He looked out the window and stuck his tongue out again as another car drove by.

Jeremy held up a camera. "Hey, George, say cheese."

George made a funny face as Jeremy snapped a photo.

"What was that for?" George asked him.

"I'm taking pictures of our field trip for the *Class 3A Times*," Jeremy explained. He was editor of the class newspaper.

"Cool, how about this one?" George asked. He stood up and held his ears straight out as a car passed by.

"Mrs. Derkman will be really mad," Katie reminded them.

George sighed. "Katie Kazoo, you're a goodie-goodie!" he exclaimed.

"I am not!" she insisted.

"You are, too," George told her. "You never

get in trouble. You never do anything wrong. You're a goodie-goodie."

"Goodie-goodie," Kevin repeated. "Katie is a goodie-goodie."

"Katie is a goodie-goodie," Manny joined in. "Katie is a goodie-goodie."

The boys' chanting grew louder and louder. Katie's face got redder and redder. She was mad. And she was hurt, too. After all, Katie and George were friends. She'd been the first one to be nice to him when he was the new kid at school. And George was the one who had given Katie her way-cool nickname, Katie Kazoo.

But George sure wasn't treating Katie like a friend right now. He kept on singing, "Katie is a goodie-goodie, Katie is a goodie-goodie."

"That's enough!" Mrs. Derkman shouted from the front of the bus.

The boys quieted down right away.

"It's almost the end of the school year. By now, I would expect you to know how to act

on a field trip. If you children cannot behave, I will ask Mr. Bloom to turn this bus around right now. We can go back to school and have a math test instead of a field trip," Mrs. Derkman warned.

Suzanne looked at Katie. "See, I told you boys were rotten!"

"George was mean. And he was wrong. I'm not a goodie-goodie," assured Katie.

"Well . . ." Suzanne said slowly. "Not all the time, anyway."

"What's that supposed to mean?" Katie asked her.

"Nothing," Suzanne said. "It's just that you hardly ever get in trouble."

"I do, too," Katie insisted.

"When?"

"There was that time Mrs. Derkman read our note out loud," Katie said. "We got in trouble then."

"That was months ago," Suzanne reminded her. "And I was the one who sent the note in

the first place. You were just answering me."

"How about the time Mr. Kane caught me with a cell phone?"

Suzanne laughed. "Me again. It was *my* cell phone, remember? I brought it to school. You were just holding it when Mr. Kane walked into the cafeteria."

Katie looked across the aisle at Jeremy. "You don't think I'm a goodie-goodie, do you?"

Jeremy didn't answer.

"Jeremy," Katie insisted.

"It's okay to be a goodie-goodie," Jeremy said finally. "Everybody has to be something. George is funny. Kevin is the Tomato Man. I'm good at sports . . ."

"I'm fashionable," Suzanne added. "Mandy's really smart. Zoe's an artist . . ."

"And you're a goodie-goodie," Jeremy finished. "It's just who you are."

"We like you anyway," Suzanne said.

Katie frowned. Somehow, that didn't make her feel any better.

Chapter 2

As the bus rolled along, Katie stared out the window. She tried not to think about what her friends had said. But she couldn't help it. Especially since George and Kevin kept whispering, "Goodie-goodie, goodie-goodie," into her ear.

Katie wanted to ask Mrs. Derkman to make them stop. But telling on the boys would only make her seem like more of a goodie-goodie.

The truth was, George couldn't be more wrong. Katie had actually gotten into trouble lately. Lots of trouble.

In the past few months, Katie had wound

up in the boys' locker room, started a food
fight in the cafeteria, and completely ruined
Becky's report on Cleopatra. She'd also
wrecked part of Mrs. Derkman's prized garden.
George would have loved to have seen that!

But none of Katie's friends knew about
the trouble she had gotten into.

How could they?

All those things had happened when Katie
had magically turned into someone else. But
Katie couldn't tell her friends that. They never
would believe her. Katie wouldn't believe it
either, if it hadn't happened to her.

But it really did happen. Katie Carew turned into other people . . . a lot!

It all started one day at the beginning of the school year. Katie had lost the football game for her team, ruined her favorite pair of pants, and let out a big burp in front of the whole class. It was the worst day of Katie's life. That night, Katie had wished she could be anyone but herself.

There must have been a shooting star overhead when she had made that wish, because the very next day the magic wind came and turned Katie into Speedy the class hamster! Katie had escaped from the hamster cage, and wound up in the boys' locker room, stuck inside George's stinky sneaker! Luckily, Katie had turned back into herself before George could step on her.

The magic wind came back again and again. It turned her into Lucille, the lunch lady, and Katie had started a food fight with some really gooey egg salad. The wind had

turned her into other kids, too, like Jeremy and Becky. Once, the magic wind had even turned Katie into her very own dog, Pepper. That time, she'd chased a particularly nasty squirrel into Mrs. Derkman's yard—and had destroyed her teacher's favorite troll statue.

Katie never knew when the magic wind would come back again. All she knew was that when it did, she was going to wind up getting into some sort of trouble—and so would the person she'd turn into.

See? Katie wasn't a goodie-goodie at all.

Unfortunately, she was the only person who knew it.

Chapter 3

"Okay, class, follow me," Mrs. Derkman said as she walked up the stone staircase that led to the museum. "Remember, we have to be on our best behavior."

A tall, skinny man with a thin tuft of hair on his head walked over to greet the class. "Hello. You must be from Cherrydale Elementary School," he said.

"Yes, we are," Mrs. Derkman replied. "Are you the volunteer who will give us our tour?"

The man quickly shook his head, and pointed to a badge he wore on a chain around his neck. "I'm the Director of the Education Department," he said proudly. "But the

volunteer who was supposed to take you around called in sick. So I got stuck . . . I mean, um . . . so I got the pleasure of giving you the tour. I'm fitting you in before my next appointment. I'm going to give a very important scientist, Dr. Franklin P. Muffinstoffer, a tour of the museum."

"Oh, well . . . that's wonderful," Mrs. Derkman said. "We're very lucky to have you as our guide."

"You certainly are," the man boasted.

"I'm Mrs. Derkman," the teacher said, holding out her hand.

"I'm Mr. Weir," the man replied, shaking her hand.

"Did you hear that?" George whispered. "His name is Mr. Weird."

"He said his name was Mr. Weir," Katie corrected George.

"I don't know," Kevin said. "He looks weird to me!"

Some of the kids giggled. Mrs. Derkman

didn't. "Children!" she scolded. "This is not how we behave in a museum."

"Oh, don't worry," Mr. Weir assured her. "I can handle a bunch of children."

Katie looked over at George. She could tell he was already planning something bad to do in the museum. Suddenly, Katie felt sorry for Mr. Weir. He'd probably never met anyone like George before.

"Can we go to the Hall of Dinosaurs?" Kevin asked. "I used to go there all the time when I was little."

"When was that . . . yesterday?" Suzanne joked.

Kevin stuck his tongue out at her.

"We'll get to the dinosaurs when *I* say so," Mr. Weir said. "We're starting with the ancient Egypt exhibit."

"Do you have any real mummies in there?" George asked excitedly.

Mr. Weir shook his head. "No. Those go to the big museums in the city," he said with a

very jealous sigh. "We get stuck with the fake mummy cases."

"But they look just like the real thing," Mrs. Derkman assured class 3A.

Mr. Weir led them down a long hallway. The walls were lined with drawings made by ancient Egyptians.

"Those are called hieroglyphics," Suzanne told the others. "It's sort of a picture alphabet."

"How did you know that?" Mr. Weir asked, surprised.

"I know a lot about ancient Egypt," Suzanne told him. "I used to be Cleopatra's biggest fan. Until I got tired of her. Then I moved on to Coco Chanel. She was a famous clothing designer. And now I'm interested in learning about supermodels." She turned her face to the side. "Don't you think my bone structure is perfect?"

Mr. Weir glared at Suzanne. "Is there some way to turn her off?" he asked Mrs. Derkman.

Mrs. Derkman sighed. "Suzanne, right now we're talking about ancient Egypt," she said.

Becky Stern had been carefully studying some of the hieroglyphics on the wall. There was one picture that really interested her. It was of a man standing on his head.

Becky flipped over and stood on her hands. "Look at me!" she squealed. "I'm a hieroglyphic."

"Becky!" Katie shouted out, surprised. "Get down. You're going to break something."

"Yes, Becky," Mrs. Derkman scolded. "Get down. We walk on our feet, not our hands, in a museum."

"Katie, you're such a goodie-goodie!" Becky replied. She swung her legs down to the floor.

Unfortunately, Becky didn't see that Manny was standing right behind her. She kicked him in the stomach on her way down. Manny fell backwards and knocked over one of the three fake mummy cases. *Wham!*

Click. Jeremy took a picture of Manny, Becky, and the fallen mummy case. "That's going to be great!" he told Kevin.

Mrs. Derkman glared at Becky and Manny.

"It wasn't my fault," Manny told the teacher.

"You banged into the mummy case," Becky said.

"You banged into *me*," Manny argued.

"I told you this would happen," Katie reminded Becky.

"Be quiet, goodie-goodie," Becky said to Katie. She turned to Manny. "You want to fight about it?"

"I'd never hit a girl," Manny began. "But in your case, I could make an exception."

"Is this the kind of behavior you teach your class?" Mr. Weir asked Mrs. Derkman.

"They're just a little excited, that's all," Mrs. Derkman assured him nervously. She stood between Becky and Manny so they couldn't fight.

Bam! At that very moment, one of the still-standing mummy cases burst open. Something—or someone—leaped out at the class.

"Aaaaahhhh!" Miriam Chan screamed. "It's a mummy!" She headed for the door. As she ran, she stepped right on Mr. Weir's foot.

"Ow!" he shouted, grabbing his foot. "Darn kids!"

Suddenly, they heard some very familiar laughter. It was George. He'd been hiding in the mummy case.

"George, that was mean," Miriam shouted. "You scared me!"

"It was just a joke," George replied.

"Your behavior is not funny!" Mrs. Derkman scolded him.

"You want funny?" George asked her. "I'll give you funny. How do you make a mummy float?"

"How?" Kevin asked.

"Take two scoops of ice cream, add root

beer, then drop in a mummy!"

"George Brennan, get over here right now!" Mrs. Derkman ordered. George walked nervously over to his teacher.

"Apologize to Mr. Weir," the teacher insisted.

"I'm sorry, Mr. Weird," George said.

"It's *Weir*!" Mr. Weir shouted. "And don't you forget it!"

Chapter 4

Mr. Weir led the kids through a large open room. There was no one in there but class 3A. It was very quiet . . . until Mrs. Derkman let out a loud scream. The teacher was standing in the middle of the room, frozen in place.

"What's wrong?" Mr. Weir asked her.

Mrs. Derkman didn't say anything. She just pointed up at a massive plastic spider hanging from the ceiling. Mrs. Derkman was scared of any kind of creepy crawly creature. A giant one like that scared her even more! "W . . . w . . . what's that?" she stammered.

"Oh, that? It's a model of a tarantula," Mr. Weir answered. "Of course, a real tarantula

only has a three-and-a-half-inch body and a nine-inch leg span. This is an oversized model. We use it to point out all the interesting parts of a tarantula's body. Notice the spiny hairs that cover its middle section."

Mrs. Derkman kept staring at the giant spider hanging from the ceiling. "I had a nightmare about a tarantula once." Mrs. Derkman gulped. "It didn't end well."

As Mr. Weir talked about the spider, Mandy studied the rows of shelves in the room. They went from the floor to the ceiling. There were lots of fake insects on them.

"I bet I can climb to the top before you do," Mandy dared Jeremy.

"No way," Becky told her. "Jeremy's the best climber in the whole school." She batted her eyes at Jeremy.

Jeremy groaned.

"Come on," Mandy said. "Let's race."

"Okay, you're on!" Jeremy said.

He pulled himself up onto a shelf. Mandy

climbed up behind him.

"Look at us, we're climbing like spiders!" Jeremy called down to Katie.

Mrs. Derkman was too busy staring at the giant tarantula to notice Mandy and Jeremy climbing on the shelves. Mr. Weir was too busy listening to himself talk about spiders to even think about the kids. Mr. Weir liked the sound of his own voice.

"Get down, you guys. Someone could get hurt," Katie warned her friends.

"Katie, stop being a goodie-goodie," Mandy said.

Just then, Mr. Weir spotted Mandy and Jeremy on the shelves. "Get down from there!" he shouted.

"WHOA!!!" Jeremy lost his footing. He fell to the floor with a thud.

That made Mandy fall, too. A whole shelf's worth of plastic moths, caterpillars, flies, and worms tipped over onto her and Jeremy.

Jeremy threw his camera over to Manny.

"Quick! Take this picture," he told Manny.

"Why did I ever get out of bed this morning?" Mr. Weir groaned as the flash went off right in his eyes.

Seeing all those fake bugs on top of her students was worse than any nightmare Mrs. Derkman had ever had. "I was just thinking the same thing," she murmured.

The exhibit in the next room was of Native Americans. There was a wooden canoe in the middle of the room. Inside the canoe were four statues of Native Americans. They looked like they were paddling across a river.

"Here are some examples of Native American weaving," Mr. Weir told the class. He pointed to a glass cabinet filled with baskets and rugs.

Katie studied the baskets. They were all very pretty, with interesting patterns woven into the straw. Suddenly, she heard some of the kids behind her laughing hysterically.

Katie turned around to see what was so funny.
She couldn't believe her eyes!

George Brennan was sitting in the back of
the big canoe! He was pretending to be one
of the statues. When George saw the class
looking at him, he moved his arms back and
forth, like he was paddling the canoe. "Hey,
Kevin," George shouted out. "Can you canoe?"

"Sure," Kevin answered. "Canoe? Get it?"

The class laughed even harder. Jeremy took
a picture of George paddling in the canoe.

"Mrs. Derkman!" Katie pointed to the

canoe. "Look what George is doing."

The teacher turned around quickly. "George Brennan, you will be up the creek without a paddle if you don't get down from there right now!" Mrs. Derkman ordered sternly.

George had heard Mrs. Derkman sound like that before. He knew she meant business. Quickly, he climbed out of the canoe. Then he strutted proudly over to where Manny and Kevin were standing.

"That was classic, dude!" Manny said, giving George a high five.

Mr. Weir wiped another bead of sweat from off his forehead. "Kids," he muttered angrily under his breath.

After that, George had to walk beside Mrs. Derkman. "Thanks a lot, goodie-goodie," he whispered to Katie as the class entered the mineral and gemstone room.

"It's not my fault," Katie told him. "You were the one who climbed in the canoe."

"But you're the one who told on me," George snapped back.

"Mrs. Derkman would have seen you, anyway. Everyone saw you," Katie told him.

"This room is filled with precious and semiprecious gems. We also have ordinary minerals from all over the world," Mr. Weir told the class.

"Do you have rubies?" Miriam asked him. "That's my birthstone."

"How about diamonds?" Mandy asked.

"I know where you can find the biggest diamonds," George interrupted. "On a baseball field!"

The kids laughed.

Mr. Weir rolled his eyes and looked at his watch.

"Are there any star sapphires in your collection?" Suzanne asked. "I love them. My mother has a dark blue one that she wears on a chain around her neck. My grandmother . . ."

"How about charcoal?" Kevin interrupted.

He made his voice high and squeaky to sound like a girl's. "I adore charcoal. Look at my charcoal ring." He held out his hand to show everyone his imaginary ring.

Some of the boys started to laugh.

"Don't make fun of Suzanne," Katie said, standing up for her best friend.

"Oh, what a goodie-goodie," Kevin told her.

"I am not," Katie insisted.

"If I could actually say something . . ." Mr. Weir began.

But before Mr. Weir could finish his sentence, Manny shouted out from across the room. "Hey, you guys. Check this out!"

Everyone turned around. Manny was sitting on top of a huge slab of polished jade.

"Get down from there!" Mr. Weir shouted.

"Okay," Manny agreed. "Wheeeeeeeeee!" He slid down the slab of jade like it was the slide in the playground.

Mr. Weir took out a handkerchief and wiped the back of his neck. "Is it getting

warm in here?" he asked nervously.

"Perhaps we should try the North American Wildlife room," Mrs. Derkman suggested. She began to lead the class away from the rock and mineral room.

"I'm so mad at Manny," Miriam moaned as the class left the mineral and gemstone room. "I wanted to see a real ruby."

Katie frowned. "You were right, Suzanne," she said. "Boys can be real pains. I can't believe Manny did that."

Suzanne shrugged. "Actually, I thought he was pretty funny. But I can see why you'd be upset by it, seeing as you're a goodie-goodie and all."

Chapter 5

Suzanne's comment upset Katie. But she was even more upset about what was in the North American Wildlife room. There, the kids came face to face with bears, mountain lions, and buffalo. Unfortunately, all of the animals were dead and stuffed. They were part of giant dioramas. And, unlike the mummies, these were all real. Or, at least, they once were!

That made Katie very sad. She loved animals. She had a cocker spaniel, Pepper, who she'd raised ever since he was a pup. Katie and Pepper were always together— except when she was in school or at the mall. Dogs weren't allowed there.

Katie was also a vegetarian. She would never eat anything that had once had a face. Now, here she was in a room full of animals that had been hunted and put on display. It was awful!

Suzanne noticed that Katie was upset. "You should just walk right out of here," she told her. "It could be your way of protesting the killing of innocent animals."

Kevin overheard Suzanne. "Katie couldn't do that," he said. "She's too much of a goodie-goodie to break the rules."

Suzanne nodded. "You're right," she agreed. Then she turned to Katie. "Maybe you should just close your eyes until we leave."

Katie wasn't sure what made her angrier— the dead animals or the way her friends were teasing her about being a goodie-goodie. She had to do something. *But what?*

The class stopped in front of a stuffed brown bear. Mr. Weir began to speak. "This is the grizzly bear. It lives . . ."

Suddenly, the bear seemed to speak. "Let me out!"

Mr. Weir jumped back. "Who said that?" he demanded.

"Animals have feelings!" the bear bellowed angrily. "How would you like to be stuffed and put in here? *ROAR!*"

Just then, a little girl looking up at the bear burst into tears. "Mommy, that bear roared at me!" she cried.

The girl wasn't the only toddler in the room. Once she started crying, a pair of twin boys in a double stroller joined in. "No like bears!" one of them sobbed.

"Me, neither," cried his brother.

"WAAAAHHHHH!" The girl was really wailing now.

The sound of the shrieking toddlers really upset Mr. Weir. With each cry, his face turned redder and redder. More sweat built up on his forehead. A thick blue vein popped out on his neck.

Flash! Jeremy took a picture of Mr. Weir. "That one's a classic!" he laughed.

Mr. Weir glared at Jeremy. Then he eyed the rest of the kids in class 3A suspiciously. "Which of you *wild animals* made that bear speak?" he demanded.

George burst out laughing. "Good one, Katie Kazoo!" he cheered.

Everyone turned toward Katie. She smiled proudly.

"Katie, was that you?" Mrs. Derkman asked, surprised.

"Sure it was," George said. "She was using ventriloquism to make the bear talk. Katie's great at ventriloquism. She doesn't move her lips one bit." He turned to Manny. "Remember the time she made your backpack talk? Boy, were you freaked out!"

Manny blushed.

"I guess you're not a goodie-goodie, after all," George told Katie.

Katie smiled. Coming from George, that

was a big compliment.

"Roar!" Katie made the bear say.

"WAAAAHHHH!" cried the two-year-old girl.

"EEEYAAHHH!" screamed the twins.

Mr. Weir stuck his fingers in his ears to block out the noise.

"That's it!" he shouted angrily. "Young lady, leave this room right now."

"But, Mr. Weir," Mrs. Derkman interrupted. "I don't want to send one of my students off on her own in the museum."

"She'll be fine," Mr. Weir assured the teacher. "There are plenty of guards around. Any one of them can help her if she's got a problem."

"But . . ." Mrs. Derkman began.

"If she doesn't leave, I won't continue this tour," Mr. Weir said. "I'm tired of dealing with your students. They're acting like children."

"They *are* children," Mrs. Derkman reminded him.

"Either she leaves, or I do," Mr. Weir said angrily.

Mrs. Derkman sighed. "Katie, there's a library right down the hall. Instead of looking at the bears, you can do a small report on grizzlies. I'm sure the librarian can help you find information."

The kids all felt bad for Katie. An extra report. That really stunk!

Katie was a little sad that she would be missing the rest of the field trip. And she felt bad about scaring the little kids. But she was also proud of herself. She'd let everyone know that she thought killing animals was wrong. And she'd proved to her friends that she wasn't a goodie-goodie.

A report was a small price to pay for all that.

Chapter 6

Katie went out into the hall. She looked for a guard who could show her where the library was. But there was no one in the hallway.

Suddenly, she felt a small draft on the back of her neck. That was weird. There were no windows anywhere near her.

The draft became a breeze. Then the breeze grew stronger. Katie looked for an open window. All of the windows were shut. The breeze couldn't be coming from there, either.

Katie gulped. This wasn't any ordinary wind. This was the magic wind!

Whoosh! The magic wind picked up speed. It swirled wildly around Katie. She shut her eyes tightly and tried not to cry. The wind was big, powerful, and out of control. Katie was really scared!

But she was even more scared when the wind *stopped* blowing. She knew what that meant. The magic wind was gone . . .

And so was Katie Carew.

Chapter 7

Katie slowly opened her eyes and looked around. She wasn't in the hall anymore. The magic wind had blown her into the Hall of Dinosaurs. Everywhere Katie looked, she saw huge, prehistoric skeletons.

Okay, so now she knew where she was. But she still didn't know *who* she was.

Mandy looked up at Katie. "Was the Stegosaurus a plant-eater or a meat-eater?" she asked.

"Huh?" Katie replied.

"What did the Stegosaurus eat?" Mandy asked again.

"Um . . . let me think about that for a moment," Katie answered.

"But you're the Director of the Education Department. You should know all about this," Mandy said disappointedly.

"Stegosaurus was a plant-eater," Mrs. Derkman told her.

Katie didn't hear Mrs. Derkman's answer. She was too busy thinking about what Mandy had called her. *The Director of the Education Department?* Katie gulped. That was Mr. Weir's title!

Katie looked down at her feet. Her purple sneakers were gone. In their place was a pair of worn, black loafers. She was also wearing gray slacks and a white sweat-stained, button-down shirt. There was a badge on a chain around her neck. Katie looked at the picture on the badge. It showed a skinny man with a tuft of hair on the top of his head.

Oh, no!

The magic wind had turned Katie into Mr. Weir!

"What kind of dinosaur is this?" Manny

asked her. He was standing beside a huge, long-necked dinosaur skeleton.

Katie didn't answer. She was too busy staring at the picture on her badge. Katie felt like she was going to cry. She didn't want to be Mr. Weir. Not for one minute.

"Whoa, look at this tooth," Jeremy called out from the other side of the room. He pointed to a huge, pointy fossil. "It's as sharp as a knife."

"I wouldn't want to be his dentist," Kevin said.

"That belonged to an Allosaurus," Mrs. Derkman told the boys. "They were meat-eaters." She turned to Katie. "Mr. Weir, I think maybe there are too many children here for you. It will be easier for you to answer questions from just a few."

"Huh?" Katie murmured. She hadn't been listening to Mrs. Derkman at all.

"Sometimes, it's difficult for people who aren't teachers to handle large groups of

third-graders," Mrs. Derkman replied. "So I'm going to take some of these children into the next room. You can handle the others."

"No!" Katie shouted without thinking. She didn't want to be in charge.

"Excuse me?" Mrs. Derkman said.

Katie sighed. She had forgotten she was supposed to be Mr. Weir. "I mean, no problem," she corrected herself.

Mrs. Derkman took Jeremy, Becky, Zoe, and Manny into the next room. Everyone else stayed with Katie.

"Man, I can't believe we got stuck with Mr. Weird," Kevin whispered to Suzanne. "He hates kids."

"Would you rather be with Mrs. Derkman?" Suzanne asked him.

Kevin sighed. "I'd rather be out on the playground," he said.

Suzanne turned to Katie. "Mr. Weir," she said. "I heard the dinosaurs were all beautiful colors, like birds. Is that true?"

Katie had no idea. So she gave a Mr. Weir kind of answer. "How should I know? I'm not old enough to have been around in the time of the dinosaurs."

"I was just asking," Suzanne muttered.

"Oh, look at this one," Miriam pointed to a nest with a few eggs and some smaller dinosaur skeletons in it. "It's a baby. What kind of dinosaur is this, Mr. Weir?"

"Not a very smart one," Katie said.

"Huh?" Miriam asked.

"Any dinosaur that would have children would have to be foolish," Katie explained.

"Oh, man, this stinks!" Kevin moaned as he read one of the signs.

"What does?" Suzanne asked him.

Kevin pointed to a sign next to one of the smaller dinosaurs. "It says here that none of the dinosaur skeletons in this room are real. They're just models."

"The real dinosaurs are probably in museums in the big cities," Suzanne told him.

"Just like the real mummies. Isn't that right, Mr. Weir?"

Before Katie could answer, a loud shout came from the other side of the room.

"Yeehah! Ride 'em, cowboy!" someone yelled.

Katie turned around just in time to see George sitting on the back of a model of a huge meat-eating dinosaur!

"How did you get up there?" Kevin asked, impressed.

"I climbed up the tail," George answered. He pointed to the trail of bones that led from the floor, straight up to the dinosaur's head. "See, it's like a ladder."

"Cool. I want to try it next," Kevin said.

This was getting out of hand. Katie couldn't let the boys climb up and down on the dinosaurs. "George, get down from there right now!" she demanded.

"No way, Mr. Weird," George answered. "A cowboy doesn't get down till he's thrown from

the horse. Yeehah!" He pretended to swing an imaginary lasso.

"Please get down," Katie tried again. "You're going to get in trouble."

"That won't scare George," Suzanne told her. "He's always in trouble."

Katie reached up and tried to grab George. But George was quicker—he leaped from the dinosaur's back onto the floor. Then he ran off.

"George! Get back here!" Katie ordered. But George just kept on running. Katie followed him. Suzanne, Kevin, Mandy, and Miriam ran after Katie.

George darted into a large room. The sign on the door read "Not Open to the Public." But George didn't take the time to read the sign. He just ran right in.

Inside the room were two dinosaur models and all sorts of tools. This was the room where the museum's scientists put together the model dinosaurs. But the scientists weren't in there right now.

Unfortunately, George was.

"George! Get out!" Katie shouted as she followed him into the room.

Quickly, George climbed up the long tail of one of the dinosaurs. He sat on the dinosaur's

big head and stuck his tongue out.

That made Katie mad. She started to climb up the dinosaur's tail after George. But the fake bones couldn't hold the weight of a grown man. And that's just what Katie was at the moment . . .

CRASH!

Chapter 8

The dinosaur's tailbones collapsed to the floor like giant prehistoric dominoes. In seconds, Katie and George were sitting on the ground, surrounded by a pile of white plastic bones and wire.

"Oops," George said sheepishly.

"Oops?" Katie cried out. "Is that all you can say? Look what you've done!"

"I didn't do it. You did," George said. He rubbed his bottom. "And how come you only care about the dinosaur? I hurt my tail, too."

Katie didn't care about George's sore rear end. All she could think about was the pile of bones on the floor. Mr. Weir was going to be in

big trouble. He might even lose his job! And it would all be Katie's fault.

A tear ran down Katie's cheek.

"Whoa, check it out," Kevin said. "Mr. Weird is crying."

Katie gulped. She didn't know a lot about being the Director of the Education Department. But she was pretty sure that someone like Mr. Weir did not cry. At least, not in front of kids. Quickly, she used the sleeve of Mr. Weir's shirt to dry her eyes. "I am not crying," she corrected Kevin. "My eyeballs are just sweating."

"I've never heard of sweating eyeballs," Kevin told her.

"I believe his eyeballs are sweating. Every other part of him is sweating," Suzanne noted.

It was true. Mr. Weir's shirt was covered with perspiration. Katie felt dampness on the back of her neck and on her forehead, too. Her underarms were disgusting. Yuck. Katie frowned. Being Mr. Weir really stunk . . . in more ways than one.

Katie didn't like Mr. Weir at all. But she didn't want him to lose his job. There was only one thing to do. "We've got to put this dinosaur's tail back together," she told the kids.

"Us?" Kevin asked. "We don't know anything about being palea . . . paleee . . . pileontol . . ."

"You mean paleontologists," Mandy told him. "Dinosaur scientists."

Kevin nodded. "See, I can't even pronounce it," he told Katie. "How am I supposed to be one?"

Katie sighed. Kevin was right. They didn't know anything about being paleontologists. But they couldn't just leave that pile of bones

sitting there. They had to at least try to put the dinosaur's tail back together. "How hard can it be?" Katie asked the kids.

"Really hard," Kevin answered.

"You played with blocks when you were little, didn't you? This can't be much different. All we have to do is follow this picture." Katie pointed to a drawing of the completed dinosaur skeleton.

George picked up one of the bones. "This looks like the bottom of the tail," he said quietly.

Katie smiled at him. She could tell he was sorry for what had happened. None of his pranks had ever turned out this badly before. Maybe George would be a little more of a goodie-goodie himself after this.

"Okay," she told him. "Let's get started."

Kevin picked up a big bone. "Good thing Katie's dog's not here," he said. "Can you imagine how he'd love these things? They're huge."

"Pepper would have a lot of fun here," Katie agreed.

"Hey," Suzanne asked. "How'd you know her dog is named Pepper?"

Katie gulped. She'd forgotten she was supposed to be Mr. Weir! "I didn't," she said quickly. "I . . . uh . . . I was talking about my dog. *His* name is Pepper."

"Poor Katie," Suzanne whispered to Miriam. "First, Mrs. Derkman moves in next door to her. Now, Mr. Weir's dog has the same name as hers. Good thing she's not here to find out about that!"

Katie sighed. That was a close one.

"I'm getting hungry," George moaned.

"You're always hungry," Suzanne told him.

"Lunch isn't for another fifteen minutes," Kevin moaned as he looked at the clock on the wall.

Katie gulped. Fifteen minutes? That was hardly any time at all. They had to get the dinosaur's tail fixed before Mrs. Derkman came back. They would all be in big trouble if she found out what had happened.

"Faster, faster," Katie urged the kids. "We've got to get this thing together."

"We're almost done, Mr. Weir," Mandy said. "There's just this one big bone left."

Katie took the bone from Mandy. Quickly, she used it to attach the dinosaur to its tail. "Finished," she said, taking a deep breath.

"It looks pretty good," Kevin said. "Almost like the real thing."

"Almost?" Katie asked nervously.

"It's not like the picture," Kevin told her.

Katie looked at the picture. Oh, no! Kevin was right. In the picture, the dinosaur's tail was pointing down to the ground. Now, its tail was pointing straight out.

"Maybe no one will notice," George suggested.

"Are you kidding?" Kevin asked. "Who could miss that?"

Beep. Beep. Beep. Before Katie could say anything, she heard a strange noise coming from her shirt pocket.

Startled, Katie looked down. She reached into her pocket and pulled out a small, black

pager. She looked at the words on the screen.

COME TO YOUR OFFICE. DR. MUFFINSTOFFER HAS ARRIVED.

Katie gulped. Dr. Muffinstoffer was the famous scientist Mr. Weir was supposed to meet with. Now, Katie was going to have to be the one to show him around the museum.

But Katie didn't know anything about the museum!

This was so not good.

Chapter 9

"Um, I have to go," Katie nervously told the kids.

"You can't just leave us here," Suzanne said.

"I'll be right back," Katie said as she raced into the hall. "Don't move until I get here. And, whatever you do, *don't touch that dinosaur!*"

Katie had no idea where Mr. Weir's office could be. For a moment, she thought about asking one of the guards how to get there. But she looked like Mr. Weir now. Mr. Weir would surely know the way to his own office. If she asked for directions, the guard would surely think that Mr. Weir *was* weird.

Katie wandered around the museum until

she came to what seemed to be a row of offices. Maybe this was where Mr. Weir worked. Quickly, Katie opened the first office door and stepped inside.

Oops. This was definitely not Mr. Weir's office. Instead of a desk and books, the room was filled with mops, pails, and cleaning supplies. Katie was in the janitor's closet!

She reached for the doorknob. But before she could open the door, Katie felt a cool breeze blowing on the back of her neck. There were no windows in the closet and the door was shut tightly. Katie knew right away that this was no ordinary wind. This was the magic wind.

The magic wind grew stronger and stronger. It whirled around Katie like a tornado. Faster and faster it blew, until the wind was so strong that Katie could barely breathe.

And then it stopped. Just like that. The magic wind was gone.

Slowly, Katie opened her eyes and looked down at her feet. Her purple sneakers were back. So were her jeans. And there wasn't even a trace of sweat on her tank top.

She was Katie Carew again!

Katie knew she should find her way to the library and wait for her class. But Katie wanted to be with the rest of her class in the Hall of Dinosaurs. Unfortunately, she had no idea how to get back there.

But the real Mr. Weir certainly did.

As Katie stepped out into the hall, she found him standing outside an office door. He was staring at his beeper.

"Mr. Weir," Katie said. "What are you doing here?"

"I don't know," he mumbled. "One minute, I was in the Hall of Dinosaurs and the next thing I knew, I was standing outside of my office." He stared at Katie for a moment. "What are you doing here?"

"Um, I came to get you," Katie said quickly.

Mr. Weir didn't ask her why. He just kept staring at his beeper. "Dr. Muffinstoffer is supposed to be in my office. But I don't remember hearing my beeper or walking over here. And Dr. Muffinstoffer isn't here."

Katie didn't know what to say. She wasn't sure why Dr. Muffinstoffer had disappeared. She just hoped that it wasn't her fault. Too many things had been her fault today.

"How about we go back to the dinosaurs?" Katie said quickly.

Mr. Weir sighed. "I've got to get a new job," he moaned. "This one is too stressful."

Chapter 10

When Mr. Weir and Katie arrived in the Hall of Dinosaurs, only the kids who had been with Mrs. Derkman were there. The teacher looked frantic.

"Mr. Weir!" she cried out. "Where have you been? And where are my students?"

"I . . . um . . . er . . . I'm not certain," Mr. Weir mumbled.

Mrs. Derkman gasped. "You lost my students?"

"Well, not exactly," Mr. Weir said. "I'm sure they're around here somewhere."

"I know where they are," Katie interrupted. "Follow me."

Katie led her teacher and Mr. Weir to the back hallway and into the room where the dinosaur models were built. Sure enough, the kids were all there. So was a small man with a long white beard and glasses.

"Dr. Muffinstoffer, I can explain," Mr. Weir said as he walked over to the man with the beard. "At least I think I can . . . I'm not really sure."

"It's fine. When you weren't in your office, I started to walk around the museum myself," the famous scientist explained.

"I don't know why I wasn't there," Mr. Weir apologized. "I don't know anything."

"You can sure say that again," Jeremy whispered to George.

"Fascinating," Dr. Muffinstoffer muttered. He was looking at the tail on the dinosaur model. "I don't know how you did this."

"I'm not sure, either. It's all kind of fuzzy," Mr. Weir sighed.

"There are only a few paleontologists in

the world who are aware of the change," Dr. Muffinstoffer continued.

"The change?" Kevin asked.

"Yes." Dr. Muffinstoffer pointed to the dinosaur's tail. "This dinosaur was always thought to walk with its tail upright. Recently, we figured out that the tail stuck straight out, just like you have it here. The tail helped it balance." He turned to Mr. Weir. "But that information hasn't even been published yet. How did you know about it?"

"Well . . . I . . . I mean . . . er . . ." Mr. Weir stammered. He didn't know what to say.

"Mr. Weir knows all the up-to-date information. He rebuilt the tail himself," Katie butted in. "Some of the kids in our class helped."

"What an interesting project," Dr. Muffinstoffer said with a smile.

"There's no better way to learn about dinosaurs than to help build one, is there Mr. Weir?" Katie said.

"I, um . . . er . . . sure. I guess," Mr. Weir said. He was staring at the tail on the model dinosaur.

Jeremy pulled out his camera. "I want to get a picture of you guys with the dinosaur," he said to Mandy, Miriam, Kevin, Suzanne, and George. He turned to Dr. Muffinstoffer and Mr. Weir. "Would you be in it, too?"

"Now why would I want to . . ." Mr. Weir began angrily.

"It would be my absolute pleasure," Dr. Muffinstoffer interrupted.

"Exactly what I was going to say," Mr. Weir quickly added.

Katie choked back a laugh. That wasn't at all what Mr. Weir was going to say. He was just trying to impress Dr. Muffinstoffer.

Suzanne, George, Kevin, Mandy, and Miriam all gathered for their picture. Mr. Weir fluffed the tuft of hair on the top of his head and fixed the collar of his sweaty shirt. He wanted to be sure he looked good.

"You must really like children," Dr. Muffinstoffer said as he stood next to Mr. Weir.

"Oh, I love them," Mr. Weir said. "Ask anyone."

George was about to open his mouth to disagree, but he shut it quickly. He'd caused enough trouble for one day.

"Okay, everyone," Jeremy said. "Say dinosaur."

"Dinosaur!"

CHERRYDALE SCH

Chapter 11

"Wow! You guys were so lucky to be in Mr. Weir's group," Jeremy told George and Suzanne as he got onto the school bus behind them. "You got to *build* a dinosaur. We had to listen to Mrs. Derkman talk about them."

"We did have a lot of fun," Suzanne admitted. "Even if we were with Mr. Weird. It was a nice way to spend our last third-grade field trip."

"Yeah," Mandy chimed in. "It's hard to believe that this school year is almost over. Summer's almost here."

"My big brother Ian says fourth grade is very different than third," Kevin said

nervously. "It's a lot harder."

"Different's okay," George said. "We'll have new teachers." He didn't sound upset about that at all.

"But we won't be together," Becky Stern told the others. "There are two fourth-grade classes. Some of us will be in one class, and some will be in the other." She looked at Jeremy and sighed. She didn't want to be in a different class than him.

Jeremy rolled his eyes. *He* wouldn't mind it if he and Becky were in a different class next year.

"We can all play together at recess and after school," Katie said, trying to be cheerful. "We'll still be friends."

"Yeah, but it won't be the same," Mandy told her.

"I guess we're in for a lot of changes," Suzanne shrugged.

Just then, Katie felt a cool breeze blowing on the back of her neck. She gasped. Was it

possible that the magic wind had come to change her into someone else?

The magic wind wouldn't do that in front of other people. Or would it? Katie didn't know for sure. It was hard to say what the magic wind would or wouldn't do. She closed her eyes and got ready for the tornado to start swirling around her.

"George, close that window!" Suzanne shouted out suddenly. "The wind is ruining my hair."

Katie breathed a sigh of relief. It wasn't the magic wind, after all. It was just the breeze from an open window. "Don't worry, George, I'll close it," Katie replied.

"Ow!" Suzanne groaned. "George, stop pulling on my ponytail!"

"It wasn't me," George said. "I think it was Jeremy."

"Not me." Jeremy shook his head. "Maybe it was Manny."

Suzanne frowned and folded her arms

across her chest. "I hate boys," she sighed.

Katie laughed. Some things never changed.

Class 3A's
Dino Fun Facts

Class 3A learned a lot about dinosaurs at the museum. (Most of all, they learned never to climb on top of one!) Here are some of the fun facts they gathered on their field trip:

Dinosaurs lived everywhere! Their bones have been found all over the Earth—even in the Arctic Circle and near the South Pole.

The biggest known dinosaurs were the plant-eating Argentinosaurus huinculensis. They grew to be 115–130 feet long. They had long necks that allowed them to reach the leaves in tall trees. They also had huge tails that helped them keep their balance.

It is harder to find small dinosaur fossils than large ones. So far, the smallest known dinosaur is the Microraptor. It was only about sixteen inches long, which makes it no bigger than a crow. It was discovered in China.

The Diplodocus was the dinosaur with the longest tail. Its tail could grow to about forty-three feet long!

The deadliest dinosaurs were fast, bird-like meat-eaters. These Megaraptor, Utahraptor, and Deinonychus dinosaurs all had huge claws, sharp teeth, and wing-like arms that helped them move quickly during a chase.

The plant-eating Hadrosaurs had 960 teeth! (How'd you like to have to brush all of those?)

ᘔM

ꟄM.